William Combe

The diaboliad

The diabo-lady: A match in hell

William Combe

The diaboliad
The diabo-lady: A match in hell

ISBN/EAN: 9783337107673

Printed in Europe, USA, Canada, Australia, Japan

Cover: Foto ©Andreas Hilbeck / pixelio.de

More available books at **www.hansebooks.com**

THE
DIABOLIAD,

A

POEM.

DEDICATED TO THE

WORST MAN

IN

HIS MAJESTY'S DOMINIONS.

ALSO, THE

DIABO-LADY:

OR, A

MATCH IN HELL.

TO REIGN IS WORTH AMBITION, THO' IN HELL!—
MILTON.

LONDON:
Printed: And DUBLIN Reprinted. 1777.

DEDICATION

TO THE

WORST MAN

IN

HIS MAJESTY's DOMINIONS.

MY LORD,

I HAVE not the honour of being acquainted with your Lordship; and as I do not wish there should be any attempt to violate my property, to estrange the affections of my wife, to seduce my daughter, or corrupt my son ; it is a matter of

real

real satisfaction to me, that I have not formed any connections with you.

To addrefs you, my Lord, in the name you derive from your Anceftors, would be treating you, in common with thofe who have no titles to diftinguifh them from the herd of ordinary men. The moft eminent Bards, Orators, Philofophers, and Statefmen, have felt greater delight, and received an higher fame from titles charaƈteriftic of their excellence, than imperial favour could beftow. Does not Mr. *Garrick*'s charaƈter, my Lord, derive an honour from the application of thofe titles he fo well deferves, the *Reformer of the Stage*, the *Great Theatrical Example*, the *Britifh Aƈtor*, &c. &c. with which his particular name has no

more

more to do, than any other which has been ufed for the purpofes of focial diftinction ? If I were to quote to your Lordfhip an opinion of *Solomon's*, you might, perhaps, imagine him to be a Jew-broker, a near relation, a familiar fervant, or a character in a Comedy ; but when I mention a faying of the *Wife Man*, your Lordfhip will immediately perceive, by this diftinguifhing characteriftic appellation, that I mean no lefs a perfonage than *the King of Ifrael.* How faint does *General Sir Jeffery*, or even *Lord Amherft* found, when compared with the *Conqueror of America!* And how infipid is the title of *General, Sir William*, or even *Lord How,* on a comparifon with the *Reconquerors of it*—fhould the wifhes of Great Britain be compleated !

Cicero

Cicero and many others among the
Antients owed their names to some
personal peculiarity or defect, and
the misfortune of bandy legs gave
a well-known title to one of our own
Monarchs. I do not know, my Lord,
that Nature has been guilty of any
inattention to your form ; and if she
had, it would not have concerned
me, who look to the mind as the best
source of name and title. Though,
if I had time, and it were to the
purpose, we might find it matter of
curious speculation to enquire, why
the poorest and most ignoble man
on earth, if capricious Nature has
placed a hunch upon his back, should
be honoured with the same title as
your Lordship, and without the for-
malities of a Royal Patent.

                                  But

But to proceed.——The bulk of mankind, who are incapable of nice obfervation, and to whom, if they were capable, it would be ufelefs, look not to the more intermediate ftate of human character; but, paff-ing at once to the extremes, fix their attention on the Beft and Worft of Men. Your Lordfhip need not, therefore, be afraid, that you will efcape that celebrity which I mean to beftow by this Dedication. How-ever, not to omit any thing which may produce your conviction, I fhall beg leave, my Lord, to acquaint you, that many years ago, when mankind in general were not fo en-lightened and informed, more parti-cularly with refpect to character, as they are at prefent, a Letter was publifhed,

publifhed, addreffed *To the Moſt Im-pudent Man Living* ; a title far more vague and indeterminate than that which I have done myfelf the honour of giving to your Lordſhip. Nevcrthelefs, the public eye immediately difcovered to whom this poor performance, for it was a very poor one, was addreffed, though he was fheltered, where one would think impudence could not find a fhelter, in the bofom of the Church.

There are many in the world, who think the perfection of their abilitics to confiſt in making their viccs the means of attracting the notice of mankind. Your Lordſhip's own heart will tell you, that you are one of the number ; and furely you will think

think all further reafoning on this fubject nugatory and impertinent, when I affure you, my Lord, that your fuccefs has been equal to your wifhes.

However, if you are not convinced by my arguments; and the propriety of that title which my pen has beftowed upon you fhould be a matter of doubt in your Lordfhip's breaft; will you, my Lord, do me the favour to travel a few lines farther, and hear my excufes for the liberty I have taken? You will therefore pardon me, if I am now obliged to turn from fo important an object as Lord ——, to fo inconfiderable an Individual as myfelf.

I was

I was not born to refine and polifh my own Compofitions! The long
habit of making rapid fketches of
men and things, has rendered me
wholly incapable of filling up an
Outline with thofe effectual maffes
of light and fhade, and that happy,
harmonious mixture of colours, which
diftinguifh the woik of judicious application. I know, my Lord, that
I am a carelefs Writer : The inaccu-
racies of this Addrefs, and the pages
which fucceed it, will, I fear, fully.
prove my affertion. Neverthelefs I
feel a felf-complacency refulting from
this performance, unlaboured as it
may be, which I am fure your Lordfhip would wifh me to poffefs as
my folace and my reward. This fa-
tisfaction, therefore, I cannot fuffer
to be diminifhed, nor my allowable
                                    vanity

vanity to be mortified, by prefixing a name to my work, which is to be continually feen in the annual pages of the *blushing* Regifter, and which you never fuffer to be erafed from the Journals of your Tradefmen.

I am, my Lord, with due refpect,

Your Lordfhip's fincere Friend,

✸ ✸ ✸ ✸ ✸.

THE

THE

DIABOLIAD.

THE DEVIL, grown, old, was anxious to
    prepare
A fit Succeſſor for the Infernal Chair.
At length, he ſummon'd forth his choſen band ;
And thus the Monarch gave his laſt command :

B   " Expand

" Expand your fable wings, and fpeed to Earth !

" To every Knave of Power, and Imp of Birth,

" Statefmen and Peers, thefe welcome tidings tell,

" That I refolve to quit the Throne of HELL :

" But, ere I ceafe to reign, 'twill be my care

" From my dear Children to elect an Heir.

" For this important end, I now proclaim,

" And fwear by SATAN's high and mighty name,

" That ere the pofting Sun's refplendent ray

" Dawns on the Upper World another day,

" With all terrific pomp, I will appear

" On the dark, ebon Throne of HELL, to hear

" The Claimants of its honours each difplay

" Their-titles—to my proud, imperial fway.

" This purpofe let my favourite Mortals know,

" And give them convoy to my realms below."

They heard, and inftant foar'd upon the wind;

The Infernal Regions foon were left behind.

By

By whirlwinds borne, they urge the rapid flight,
Till, gently fluttering round the giddy height
Of PAUL's black, footy Dome, they unob-
serv'd alight.

In ftrict obedience to their King's command,
The human fhape affum'd, along the STRAND
They bend their courfe, to where the *Scaffold* ftood
That whilom fmok'd with ftreams of royal blood:
And where, I truft, if Tyrant Kings fucceed
To fpurn our facred Laws,——thofe Kings fhall
bleed.

Here they difperfe:--Some take their fav'rite way
To thofe fam'd manfions—where the Sons of Play
By trick and rapine fhare a bafe reward;
Shake the falfe dye, and pack the ready card:
In folemn tone their errand they proclaim,
Their high commiffion, and their Sovereign's name.

With

With joy and wonder ſtruck, the Parties riſe !

" Hell is worth trying for," F******** cries ;

Pigeons are left unpluck'd, the game unplay'd,

And F—— forgets the certain Bett he made ;

E'en S--l--n feels Ambition fire his breaſt,

And leaves, half-told, the fabricated Jeſt.

Well-pleas'd, th' Infernal Miniſters reſume

Their real forms, and through the midnight gloom,

On wide-ſtretch'd wings, the eager Claimants bore

To the dank darkneſs of the Stygian ſhore.

The reſt of Hell's induſtrious Band reſort

To the corrupted Purlieus of the Court ;

To lure the Stateſman from his deep-lay'd ſcheme,

To weak the Courtier from his golden dream,

And make the C—b—l—n deſire to hold

Hell's weighty Sceptre,—for 'tis made of gold.

Sure he'd reſign for ſuch a tempting fee !

HELL's Sceptre far outweighs the Golden Key !

But

But cautious H ******* fhrinks, when rifks
　　are run,
And leaves fuch Honours for his ELDEST SON.

Now prowling onwards to the noifome caves
Where PROSTITUTION rules her needy flaves,
They tempt the Lordling, by Ambition's charms,
From the rank pleafures of a Harlot's arms ;
Then, with the Mortal Croud, they bend their
　　flight
To the dark realms of everlafting Night.

Lords of the Chamber,—Minifters of State, ⎫
With Sons of Lords, and Hirelings of the Great ; ⎬
Men whom the Villain only loves, the Worthy ⎭
　　hate ;
Follow'd by Pimps, Bawds, Parafites and Whores,
In crouds, approach'd Hell's adamantine doors.

　　　　　　　　　　　　As

As they came onward, MERCURY the gay *
With lively greetings met them on the way ;
He was the brisk Sir *Clement Cotterell* of the day.

The

* If the Orthodox Critic fhould here obferve, that I have
thrown a flight upon *his* Devil, by introducing fo great
an Heathen as *Mercury* to his employment, he will dif-
cover, when he lowers his eyes to this part of the page,
that I have made the obfervation before him.——But,
if according to fome of the ancient Chriftian Fathers,
his *Satanic Majefty* was fuppofed, for his own private
ends, to concern himfelf with the Heathen Oracles,
Sybils and Pythoneffes, I may, furely, under their re-
fpectable authority, make him have occafional recourfe
to another of the fame family, without the leaft de-
gradation. Befides, I had not one of the Rabbinical
Writers within my reach, while I was writing this
Poem, to give me the name of SATAN's Gentleman
Ufher: fo that, to fave myfelf trouble, which I
at all times hate and deteft, I borrowed an ac-
quaintance from the Grecian Poets.——Again, if my
Critic will but confider of whom the troop confifted
which received fafe conduct from this winged guide,
he muft efteem *Mercury*, who is, (Heathenly fpeaking)
the prefiding Genius of rogues, fharpers, &c. as properly introduced to be their conductor.——And as an
Orthodox Critic muft confider all fuch in the light of
Heathens, my application to the Pagan Mythology will
not appear fo *mal aprepos* as he at firft imagined.

The winged God thrice wav'd his magic wand!

The maffive doors acknowledg'd his command ;

And, to the Claimants wond'ring Eyes, difplay'd

SATAN in all his gloomy pomp array'd.

High, in his throne, on golden columns rear'd,

The venerable King of Hell appear'd.

In his right Hand a weighty mace he bore,

And on his brow a regal crown he wore ;

Begirt around with fpiral flames, which fhed

A filver luftre o'er his aged head.

Beneath the Throne, arrang'd in order, fat

The long eftablifh'd Council of the State.

In every hand the flaming torches wave,

And caft their fplendor through th' imperial cave.

High in the vault the fiery Dragons fhone,

And Monfters, whofe dire fhape was never known

To mortal fantafy,—when, Reafon flown,

Fear fills the mind with fpectres of her own.

With flaky flames the diftant region glow'd,

Whofe angry light, in all their horrors, fhew'd

Thofe

Thofe fields of fire where guilty Spirits dwell,
And in loud ceafelefs fhrieks their anguifh tell,
Nor refpit know :—Hope cannot enter there,
To calm their forrows or to foothe defpair.

With horrid clangor now the clarion founds ;
Through the dark dome the jarring thunder bounds.
Then rofe the King ;—and all th' Infernal Croud
With threefold reverence to their Monarch bow'd.
Throughout the Court the expecting murmur ran,
But foon was hufh'd;—when SATAN thus began.

" Thoufands of years have pafs'd fince, firft,
    " I fell   ,
" Into the deep abyfs of flaming Hell ;
" And many an age fince my Almighty Foe
" Gave me dominion in thefe realms below.
" Ambition's Slave, from Heaven I was hurl'd
" Down to the depths of this Infernal World.
" Tho' Heaven was loft, Ambition ftill poffefs'd
" Its darling Empire in my haughty breaft.

                                    " My

" My Tribes, with fruitlefs expectation chear'd,

" And Patriot zeal, this gloomy palace rear'd—

" Here fix'd my throne,——here formed my

   " awful ftate,

" And to my will refigned their future fate.

" But, cloy'd with power, my Ambition's o'er ;

" The boafted charms of Empire are no more !

" Hear then my Children, hear your Sire de-

   " clare,

" Of Hell's dominions He fhall be the Heir,

" Whofe paft life bore the moft obdurate crimes ;

" Who gave new vigour to degenerate times ;

" Falfe to his God, who every Law defy'd,

" Thief, Traytor, Hypocrite and Parricide ;

" Let him who claims thefe Titles as his own,

" Come forward, prove his claim,——and take

   " the crown."

The Monarch ceas'd !—F * * * foremoft ftood

And wav'd his hand to hufh the murmuring croud.

       Then

Then graceful bow'd around; but, ere he fpoke,
Satan again the awful filence broke:

" Well--meaning Youth ! thy great and noble
    " aim
" Deferves remembrance in the rolls of Fame !
" But know, for to thyfelf 'tis yet unknown,
" Thefe Characters of Ill thou canft not own.
" Within the deep receffes of thy breaft
" The pregnant feeds of many a virtue reft.
" Now baneful paffions do their place fupply,
" And check their progrefs to maturity.
" The feverifh ardor of difaftrous Game
" Burns with a furious, unrelenting flame ;
" And daily feeks to quench its parching thirft
" By deeds efteem'd the nobleft and the firft
" In Hell's black Calendar.—The foul defign
" To make another's wealth, by treachery, thine;

To

" To charm, with pleafing arts, the artlefs Heir,

" To call thee friend,——then lay th' un-

     erring fnare,

" Pocket his fleeting gold,——and leave him

     " to defpair.

" But I, who every diftant Age can fee,

" Whofe keen look kens the vaft Futurity,

" Ill-pleas'd thy alter'd character behold,

" No more by hungry Appetites controll'd ;

" From every hateful vice and paffion free,

" Lov'd by the Gods above—and loft to Me !

" Farewel !——Thy well-meant efforts will be

     " vain !

" Cherubs attend to bear thee back again!"

In order due, VOLPONE next appear'd ;

Loofe was his hair, unfhaven was his beard :

O'er his whole face was fpread a yellow hue,

Borrow'd, perhaps, from fome relenting Jew

                                Not

Not anxious to be paid.—Gold he had none;

Th' inverted pocket told that all was gone.

But ere he made his claim to Hell's rewards,

His right hand wav'd aloft the fatal Cards.

Then, fmiling, thus he fpoke:——" All-gracious
      " power !

" Who from my natal to the prefent hour,

" Didft o'er my life, with foftering care, prefide,

" My Friend, my Guardian, and my faithful
      " Guide !

" How weak the Tafk my Actions to review !

" You know them all, dread Sir, they fprung
      " from You !

" And now, I truft, 'tis You alone fuggeft

" The great, determined purpofe of my breaft,

" To try my chance, at this important hour,

" And *ftake my Soul* againft your fov'reign
      " power—

                      " Who

" Who wins have both."——" Thy foul's al-
    " ready mine,"
SATAN replied :—" and I this day affign
" Thy earthly duty.—Hence, begone, to bait,
" With maftiff zeal,—a Minifter of State."

" Poor C——— difmifs'd, next comes a noble
    Peer,
Grooms, Pimps, and Link-boys, give the triple
    cheer.
His right hand bore a Horfe-fhoe and a Bit ;
His left, a Book by *Angelona* writ ;
To whofe fair pages—anxious after fame,
His Lordfhip ventur'd to prefix his name.
A Wife complain'd that matrimonial dues
Were nightly wafted in the wanton ftews ;
A Friend lamented how he was beguil'd,
And mourn'd a ruin'd and forfaken Child ;

                        While

While two attendant Parfons boldly fwore,

They never wanted—but he paid the Whore:

Then loud proclaim'd his knowledge in the
　　wiles

Of drabby *Drury* and of low St. *Giles.*

E'en Saint-like GODBY blafts her eyes, and
　　fwears,

P * * * * 's the moft abandon'd of his Peers *.

　　　　　　　　　　　　　　　　　His

* This noble perfon, verging to that time of life when he may fay of the Brothels, " I myfelf have no pleafure " in them," is fond of introducing Gentlemen of the Black Cloth and Character into thefe places, where he enjoys the contemplation of their pleafures, and pays for them. *Mrs. Godby*'s piety fuffers very much upon thefe occafions, and can only be equalled by his L * * * * * 's refinement, which is fo univerfally known, that I expect every day to hear of its being fnug in a proverb.

It is not impoffible that the fcene of the two M—ls—ts, Father and Son, may be acted over again, and again, when a certain young Nobleman returns from his travels.

　　　　　　　　　Godby's Noclurnals, p. 116*.*

　　　　　　　　　　　　　　　N. B. The

His Vouchers done, with simper on his cheek

He silent stood ;——for P * * * * * * * cannot

    speak;

When the sage Council, with one voice de-

    clare——

" Rough-riders would disgrace *a regal Chair.*"

Without one Virtue that can grace a name;

Without one Vice that e'er exalts to Fame;

The despicable B * * * * * * * next appears,

His bosom panting with its usual fears :

He strives in vain,—and fruitless proves the art,

To hide, with vacant smile, the treacherous

    heart.

                      The

N. B. The manuscript from which this last note is taken, will make its appearance in due time, and unfold some transactions which the world little thinks of.

The faithful HARRY * ſtands not by his ſide,

His learned Counſel, and his conſtant guide ;

.

Who

* This young Nobleman's character is, in every re-
ſpect, a ſtriking contraſt to his ———— ; but the following
Anecdote will give a very ſtrong explanation of my idea
concerning him.—When Mr. C—— F—— propoſed him
tb be elected into one of the faſhionable clubs, he was
almoſt univerſally black-balled. Mr. F——, who *at
that time* had great intereſt there, was much ſurpriſed that
his friend ſhould be thus rejected : But as he concluded,
and not without reaſon, that the univerſal diſguſt in
which the family of his Friend was held had prevented
his ſucceſs, he propoſed him again, with a declaration,
on his honour, that Mr. C · · · · had not one quality in
common with any of his family. The event juſtified
Mr. F——'s penetration, on the ſecond Ballot not a
ſingle black-ball appeared againſt his friend.————
This Anecdote has been aſſerted to me as fact : But be
that as it may, the principle of it is founded in truth, and
ſerves the purpoſe of doing juſtice to a moſt amiable Character, whoſe great merit the Author of theſe pages, who
ſincerely loves him, is glad to atteſt.

Who for an hard earn'd, narrow compelence,

Supplies his tongue with words, his head with

     fenfe †.

At length, recovered from his huge affright,

He, ftammering, reads the Speech he did not

     write :

   " Curft with hereditary love of pelf,

" I hate all human beings but myfelf;

             C   " Crofs

---

† It is not uncommon for an avaricious Father to fad-
dle a younger Brother for a maintenance on the elder,
efpecially if he has a place. And if the latter fhould
poffefs an hereditary bafenefs, he will carry on the fpirit of *conditionalizing*, and infift that the former fhall,
in return, give him the ufe of his underftanding. It
too often happens that elder brothers want fpirit and
underftanding, and that younger ones who have both
in an eminent degree, ftand in need of a provifion. It
is hard that Worth and Genius fhould be fo fituated !
but this is among the fore evils under the Sun !

" Crofs and perplex my wife, becaufe fhe

     prov'd,

" Poor girl!—not rich enough to be belov'd.

" But all return my hate :—where'er I go,

" My coward eye beholds a ready foe.

" And tho' to Earth's extremes my feet. I

     " bend,

" Thefe arms would ne'er embrace a real

     " friend.

" When my breaft throbs with unrelenting

     " grief,

" No friendly Spirits bring the kind relief.

" If I fink down beneath oppreffing pain,

" Surrounding foes rejoice as I complain.

" I'm fcoff'd by thofe, who from my hand

     " have prov'd

" That kindnefs which would make *another*

     " lov'd;

                      " Men,

" Men, who to other Patrons bend their
    " knee,

" Are proud of their Ingratitude to me.

" Thus, without Friends on earth, I humbly
    " fue

" To find, my gracious Liege, a Friend in
    " you.

" *Hated by all,*—I'm fit to be allied

" To your Imperial State!"——The King re-
    plied :

    " If vacant fmiles and hypocritic air

" Could form pretenfions to this fov'reign
    " Chair ;

" If my pale Crown by *meannefs* could be
    " won,

" Who'd have fo fair a claim as H * * * * * * *'s
    " Son ?

" But

" But Meanneſs is a Vice which Devils diſ-
        " dain !

" Should'ſt thou attempt, baſe Mortal, here
        " to reign,

" To wield this Sceptre,—and to wear my
        " Crown;

" Th' infernal Hoſt would riſe to caſt thee
        " down,

" With furious zeal, where outcaſt Spirits
        " lie,

" In the dark dens of gnaſhing Infamy.

" Such minds as thine,—Obſerve the truth I
        " tell !

" *Find neither Friends on Earth,—nor Friends*
        " *in Hell.*

                                Appall'd

Appall'd the haplefs Lordling fneak'd away,

And Harpies hifs'd him to the realms of Day *.

The

* Several of my friends who were kind enough to approve, and, indeed, enforce the publication of this little Work, feemed to think that I had fruftrated my intention of marking the infignificance of this Character, by giving fo many lines to the delineation of it. But as the bold ftrokes are more eafily imitated than the finer pencillings of nature, thofe colourlefs bad qualities which have not fufficient ftrength or fpirit to rife into daring, manly vice, require a great length of defcription to imprefs them properly on the attention of the Reader. Indeed, it is my ferious opinion, that this man's life would be a profitable leffon to the world, to prove, that *meannefs of fpirit*, though unaccompanied by any bold, open violations of virtue, will ever be more contemptible, obnoxious, and diftreffing, than any of thofe public vices which are feldom wholly unconnected with fome fort of principle, and often originate from the fame fource with many virtues. The ebullitions of youth, the fpur of neceffity, the prevalence of example may hurry to enormities. In thefe cafes, however, the caufe is not always difficult to be removed, and frequently removes itfelf. The effects will then ceafe, and honour and virtue return.

But

The murmurs hufh'd,—the Herald ftraight
    proclaim'd

S--L--N the witty next in order nam'd.

                    But

    But a mean fpirit, as in this example, is a low, fneaking, bafe, fixed propenfity to what is bad, which it loves; and yet is compelled by its fears to affume the femblance of good, which it hates. It is wholly incorrigible, and attends the Character it has once poffeffed through every degree of ftation and of life; and is very feldom or never known to rife into momentary courage or fpirit; unlefs fuicide, to which it has fometimes applied for a difmiffion from univerfal contempt, may be confidered as examples of them.

    But this fubject, which I have already extended beyond the limits of a note, fhall be confidered in a feparate publication, illuftrated and proved by anecdotes of the Character before me when he was at School, the Univerfity, in France, Ireland, Warwickfhire, and London; as a School-boy, a Collegian, a Traveller, a Secretary, a Militia-commander, a Hufband, and fo on to the prefent times,—with collateral relations.

But He was gone to hear the difmal yells

Of tortur'd Ghofts and fuffering Criminals.

Tho' fummon'd thrice, he chofe not to re-

    turn,

Charm'd to behold the crackling Culprits

    burn.

With GEORGE, all know Ambition muft give

    place,

When there's an *Execution* in the cafe. *.

                        Then

---

* I would not be guilty of injuftice to any Character. *George* does not want humanity! nay, he has an un-common portion of this virtue: it extends even to the *gallows*; and is well known to have bedewed his cheeks with tears at the lamentable fate of that *pious perfonage*, commonly called, *Sixteen-String Jack*. And I may venture to affert, that he never faw a man hang'd in his life, but when the *fport was over*, he would have been really happy to have reftored him to life. It requires a kind of knowledge which every-body does not poffefs, to reconcile the apparent contradictions in

                      the

Then in Succeſſion came a Peer of words,

Well known—and *honour'd* in the *Houſe of*

Lords,

Whoſe

the human character. However, I ſhall not, at preſent,
enter further upon the ſubject than to obſerve, that
there are certain propenſities in the mind, which, being
long indulged, become irreſiſtible, and ſtand between
Men and their beſt intereſts. All the World knows
that Mr. S—— is attached to gaming, and that when
he games, he wiſhes to win. And there are many will
tell you, that this love of play, when it has taken root,
becomes the leading, if not the ſole, propenſity of the
human breaſt. But in the Character before me, there
is an evident example of two leading propenſities in the
ſame mind, which, upon certain occaſions, form a ſpi-
rit of accommodation, and blend with each other. This
very Gentleman, though he had made a very conſi-
derable bet that he ſhould not be at a certain execution,
was, notwithſtanding, diſcovered to be actually preſent at the *ſpectacle*, dreſſed like an old woman, in a
joſeph and bonnet, and ſeated on horſeback, &c. &c.
This is a twofold irreſiſtible propenſity! Nevertheleſs,
George is a man of humanity.

Whofe Eloquence all Parallel defies !

So SANDWICH fays, and SANDWICH never

lies.

No doubt, the partial Earl delights to fee,

In this young Lord, his own Epitome,

Behind him came, in Regimentals dreft,

The brazen *Gorget* hanging on his breaft,

Th' obfequious Coufin, ready to obey,

Whate'er might be the bufinefs of the day.

With folemn look the confcious Peer began

Thus to addrefs the *Military Man :*

" Friend, Coufin, Pimp, or by whatever

" name

" You would be *blafted* by the trump of

" Fame,

" Approach, and lend me now unufual aid !

" You, my brave Soldier, never are afraid,

" But

" But when the critic brows of Ladies frown :

" With thy affiftance, I fhall mount the
    " Throne;

" And then, to thee, my Coz, thefe Powers
    " fhall bend,

" Their Monarch's favourite Counfellor and
    " Friend.

    " Oft at thy curious vice I've ftood a-
    " maz'd,

" While *half-fledg'd Subalterns*, with wonder,
    " gaz'd.

" Of you, their fage *Lieutenant, Enfigns* learn

" The weaknefs of all Virtue to difcern !

" You fill their brains with Honour and Re-
    " nown;

" And teach them how to live——*upon the*
    " *Town;*

                                    " To

" To whore, to bully, to blaſpheme, to

    " game,

" To ſcorn the boyiſh bluſh and honeſt

    " ſhame ;

" And having vers'd them in each common

    " evil,

" Lead them to Maſques to perſonate the

    Devil :

" Their grateful Parents will your pains re-

    " quite,

" And fill the Boxes on an Author's Night.

" 'Twas you unlock'd a pious Parent's doors

" For Panders, Gameſters, Whores, and Sons

    " of Whores ;

" And, with uncommon filial duty bleſt,

" Sent her from Hell on earth, in Heaven to

    " reſt.

                         " But

" But to my purpofe.——— In the world
       " above,

" Bound by refembling charaɛters and love,

" We liv'd together, and together ſtray'd

" In Vice's public walk and fecret ſhade.

" I found thee apt in every artful wile,

" Proud to defame, and eager to beguile.

" Whene'er I figh'd to praɛtiſe a Deceit,

" In thee, my Coz, I found the ready Cheat.

" Whene'er I wanted Falfehood to fupply

" The place of Truth,—you found the ready
       Lie.

" When, to give fpirit to fome tedious hour

" I wifh'd to fee the Pedant Parfon lower,

" To make the Simple ſtare, the Virtuous
       " figh,—

" Your tongue pour'd forth the ready Blaf-
       " phemy.

                          " But

" But now the fcene is chang'd ; that farce is
   " o'er,

" And e'en your Falfehood will affift no more.

" Start not at what I fay,——well-temper'd
   " Youth !

" Be not alarm'd,—you now muft fpeak the
   " truth.

" Look not fo pale, 'twill fuit your nature
   " well;

" You *ly'd on Earth*, and you *fpeak truth in*
   " *Hell*."

This chear'd him much, and made his cheeks
   to glow,

And fav'd his bofom from the threat'ning
   woe ;

Which when his Lordfhip faw, in haughty
   tone

He thus laid claim to the Infernal Throne.

        " Is

" Is there a guilty deed I have not done?

" What fay you, Coz.?" The Captain an-

        fwer'd, " None!"

" Have I not whor'd myfelf, and made thee

        ", whore?

" Confirm it with an oath!"—The Captain

        fwore.

", Have I not acted every Villain's part?

" Have I not broke a Noble Perent's heart?

" By deeds of ill have I not feem'd to live?".

The Captain gave a bold affirmative.

" Do not I daily boaft, how I've betrayed

" The tender Widow, and the virtuous Maid?

" Thefe ferious crimes you know, and many

        " more:

" Swear, Sir!"—By *Egypt's* *Queen* the Cap-

        tain fwore !

                                        (The

(The Queen who lur'd him to difgrace his
    cloth,
And gave him bread, now ferv'd him for an
    oath).

But as he fpoke, there iffued from the
    croud,
* * * * * * the bafe, the cruel, and the proud;
And eager cried, " I boaft fuperior claim
" To Hell's dark Throne, and * * * * * * is
    " my name.
" What, fhall that ftripling Lord contend
    " with me ?
" I have four Sons as old and bad as he !
" Whate'er he fwears, I'll fwear—he fays, I'll
    " fay !
" And look, All-gracious King, *my hairs are*
    " *grey !*"

                        Th'

Th' aftonifh'd Demons on each other gaz'd,

And SATAN's felf fat filent and amaz'd ;

Revolving, in his dubious mind, the ftate

And crimes of each afpiring Candidate ;

When clanking chains, and doleful fhrieks were

   heard,

And injur'd * * ~~Harry~~'s raving Ghoft ap-

   pear'd * :

His bofom heav'd with many a torturing figh,

And bloody ftreams gufh'd forth from either

   eye.

          With

 * See the *Letters of Junius*, where that able Writer
has obferved, with his ufual fpirit and good fenfe, upon
this guilty tranfaction. *Junius* felt for human nature,
and would not fuffer his pen to trace all the particulars
of it. To degrade the Criminal, they fhould be re-
membered ; but for the fake of humanity, they had
better be forgotten.

With piteous look he did a Tale unfold,

Black with such horrid deeds, that, being told,

Hell's craggy vaults with acclamations ring,

And joyful shouts of ~~Hardja~~* * shall

    be King!"

the 8

King of eng

and

F I N I S.

T H E

D I A B O - L A D Y.

THE
DIABO-LADY:

OR,

A MATCH IN HELL.

A

POEM.

DEDICATED TO THE

WORST WOMAN

IN

HER MAJESTY'S DOMINIONS.

O Faireſt of Creation, laſt and beſt
Of all God's works, creature in whom excelled
Whatever can to ſight or thought be formed,
Holy, divine, good, amiable, or ſweet!
How art thou loſt !

MILTON.

LONDON:

Printed: And DUBLIN Reprinted. 1777.

DEDICATION

TO THE

WORST WOMAN

IN

HER MAJESTY's DOMINIONS.

MADAM, or, MY LADY,

AS I am happily but little acquainted with Ladies in high life, I confefs myfelf perfectly ignorant · either of your rank or demerits; which

which has reduced me to the auk-ward neceffity of this vague and in-definite addrefs. The character above defcribed will, no doubt, be feverally and particularly applied, according to the World's guefs, knowledge, or malevolence; and a certain confcioufnefs in fome female breafts, may poffibly make them conclude themfelves to be the per-fons obliquely aimed at in this place; but I hereby declare, that I had no fpecific Female in view when I fat down to write this Dedication; and fhall therefore refer my fair Readers to the known Adage of, *Qui capit, ille fecit;* which, for their fakes, I fhall tranflate, by a fynoni-

mous

mous Englifh Proverb, *Whom the Cap fits, e'en let them wear it.*

The following Verfes, be affured of it, Madam, are the firft *Juvenalian* Lines ❦ ever compofed, in my life; but being a fort of Knight-errant in my Nature, I confefs I felt myfelf confiderably piqued, for the honour of your fex, upon perufing a Poem called *The* DIABOLIAD, lately publifhed; and not feeing any manner of reafon, why or wherefore Women have not as good a right, where equal merits appear, to be *damned to everlafting fame*, as well as Men, I have thus boldly ventured to enter the lifts

lifts of Chivalry againſt that partial Author, and meaſure my lance with his, in the extenſive *Campus Martius* of Satire.

" Tremble, thou wretch !
" That haſt within thee undi-
      " vulged crimes,
" Unwhipt of juſtice!"

We neither of us pretend to ſtile ourſelves Poets (I ſpeak for my-ſelf, at leaſt); ſo that to carry on the alluſion above made, we may be conſidered rather as *Squires*, than *Knights*, in this ſpecies of literature. But as Indignation is ſaid to in-
ſpire

fpire Verfe, we have equally, and I think commendably too, expreffed our refentment againft the numerous vices and grofs immoralities of the times.

The example of Superiors is a a matter of great moment to the inferior claffes of mankind. The vices of the Great naturally defcend; but thofe of the Vulgar feldom rife. People of rank muft ftoop to them, ere they receive the infection. The depravity of a fingle Peer or Peerefs, about St. James's, diffufes more poifonous effects thro' the Town, than all the profligacy of St. Giles's.

Poffibly,

DEDICATION.

Possibly, the corrupt manners of the present age may not exceed those of former times ; but there is this peculiar distinction to be observed between them, that, upon a comparison, the purity, virtue and decorum, of our King and Queen form so striking a Contrast with the Corruption of manners among the generality of our Nobility, and other respectable ranks of life, in this kingdom, as may render the Modern Libertinism and Indecencies of this Nation, more apparently remarkable, than those of our Predecessors. Charles and his Court were of a Piece——— George and his are of a quite different Pattern.

The

DEDICATION.

The ftricteft and moft compre-
henfive laws of Men, cannot be
fo aptly framed as to apply a re-
medy, or 'fcourge, to many of the
crimes and enormities daily prac-
tifed in the world. Satire, therefore, is an ufeful Supplement to
legiflation. When a Culprit ef-
capes out of the hands of juftice,
he fhould always be hanged in
effigy. This refource, then, in
fome fort, ferves to fupply the Office of CENSOR, which it was
thought neceffary to eftablifh in
the antient Common-wealth of
Rome.

The fharp pen of Aretin once
made moft of the Sovereign Princes
of

of Europe his tributaries; and the keen Iambics of Archilochus and Hipponax, who, without vanity I may fay, were not better Poets than we, are faid to have driven the perfons who were the fub-jects of them, to fuch acts of defperation, as to hang and drown themfelves. I fhould be forry to hear of fo tragical an effect being produced by the lines of my fpi-rited Compeer or me; for though I bear hatred to vice, I harbour no malevolence, even to the vi-cious; but if our ftrictures fhould conduce towards the reformation, the contrition, or repentance, of the feveral objects of our reproof, we may be faid to have perform-

ed

DEDICATION.

ed some service, at least, to the Common-wealth of Morals. Such as they are, you are most heartily welcome to them ; and that you may receive the full benefit of their intention is the sincere wish of,

MADAM, or, My LADY,

Your most humble

And obedient Servant,

BELPHEGOR.

DEDICATION

ADVERTISEMENT.

BY THE

EDITORS.

WHEN the following Poem was put into our hands, we thought it neceſſary to write Notes on ſome of the paſſages, in order to render the Text more clear and intelligible ; for though the Author, in his Preface, takes the liberty of comparing himſelf to *Juvenal*, we are of opinion that he more reſembles *Perſius* ; whoſe writings are both more ſevere, and obſcure. But in ſome places, indeed, he has ſpoken rather too plain ; which has induced us to leave out ſeveral of his lines, as may be ſeen by the aſteriſks, in ſome of the following pages.

E

THE

DIABO-LADY.

A

POEM.

THE

DIABO-LADY.

Nec tibi regnandi veniat tam dira cupido;
Quamvis Elysios miretur Græcia campos,
Nec repetita sequi curet Proserpina matrem.

VIRG. Georg. I.

* * now seated on the Infernal Throne, (*a*)

Thought it not good the DEVIL should be alone;

And

(*a*) See The Diaboliad, last line.

' And so resolved to marry, if a Wife,

Fit Consort, could be found, to match his life.

" Shall I, said he, who ne'er obeyed a God,

" Observe his precepts in my own abode ;

" Restrain my acts within the Christian scope,

" And whore in celibacy, like the POPE ?

. " What tho' I'm head of that Hierarchal

" Scheme,

" Which deems it sin in Priest to quench their

" flame

" In Marriage rites ; yet Modern Records tell,

" Tho' made in Heaven, they are confirmed in

" Hell.

" Since such the present state of Wedlock, I,

" As Priest and Devil, will the adventure try.

" Besides the Pagan system is my Creed,

" And in that antient ritual all may read,

" That

" That Pluto our great Prototype, had wed

" A mortal female to his throne and bed." (*b*)

He faid ; then fent his Imps thro' Earth to

    rove,

And chufe a Paramour for SATAN's love

The ready Minifters of Hell's commands

Obedient fly, and take their feveral ftands

At COURT, CORNELY's, and the COTERIE ;

Where Vice, more vicious by effrontery,

Fearlefs, unblufhing, braves the eternal laws

                      Of

(*b*) The Poet may poffibly be reprehended here, by fome Critics or Divines, for the confufion of theology that may be objected to this paffage. But as the good old proverb fays, that *Example is better than precept*, we fhall refer his defence, firft, to Ariflo, or Taffo, I forget which, for I am but a poor fcholar in the *baftard Latin* Authors, where the Heathen mythology and the Chriftian fyftem are mixed together in the fame fcene ; and, next, to Rubens, who in his Luxemburgh Gallery has made Hymen and St. Denis (I think it is) jointly prefide at the marriage of Henry IV.

Of GòD and MAN, to aid the DEVIL's caufe.

From thefe reforts the Imps of SATAN chofe

So hopeful a Seraglio, that 'twould pofe

The DEVIL himfelf to judge the equal claims

To Hell's Sultanafhip, between fuch Dames ;

Who eager all to obtain Infernal fway,

In order thus prefer their feveral plea.

Firft * appeared, and to conviction fwore,

Her fmalleft crime was that of being Whore ;

Adultery fhe added to her plan,

Defying equally both GOD and Man ;

In forgery and perjury owned fuch art,

She palmed the Gold, while others paid the

      fmart :

And left her juft pretences fhould be vain,

The *Adelphi* P * * (c) vouch the tragic fcene.

SATAN

(c) Sir T * * F * * too might have fufficiently fup-
ported the fame evidence ; but, by his not being mentioned in this caufe, 'tis to be fuppofed that his avocations
in 'Change-Alley had prevented his appearance *yet* in

SATAN. with pleasure heard the shocking tale,

But inward grieved such merits there should fail;

" The Vice defeats itself," replied the DEVIL,

" That makes *examples* to deter from evil."

Next * * forward came, as frail as fair,

And urged her suit with confidential air :

" Tho' nobly born," she cried, "and high in life,

" A spotless Maiden, and an honoured Wife,

" Yet scorning these, I spurned such humble

　　" fame,

And boldly sacrificed a Matron's name :

" My first amour was with a Youth of Blood ; (d)

" But here I would not have it understood,

　　　　　　　" That

(d) Lest the equivocation of Titles might lead our readers to mistake the person, we think it proper to acquaint them that this Galant was not the hero of C * * *, but the one who going to bed *by himself*, was surprized, when he awoke, at *finding himself by himself quite alone*. See certain Love-Letters upon record.

" That 'twas Ambition made me aim so high,

. " No—'twas to aggrandize my infamy ;

" I chose, to shew all sense of virtue lost,

" A Swain who nought but pedigree could
  " boast :

" Ask treach'rous D * *, if you doubt my⎤
  " word,

" Who first abetted, then *approved* (*e*) me⎪
  " whored,   ⎬

" And stampt the shame she (*f*) had herself⎪
  " procured.   ⎦

" A first amour is seldom found the last,

" From hand to hand thro' low intrigues I
  " past ;

"   " Till

(*e*) One of the senses of this verb is, in a legal sense,
to accuse, to inform against, or convict ; from whence the
Noun *Approver*. This note had been unnecessary, if
Lexiphanes, among the other neglects in his pompous
Dictionary, had not left this article imperfect.

(*f*) A certain Lady *of quality* who was a confidant in
the amour, and afterwards proved the *Crim. Con.* in
Court.

" Till fatiating the public eye, lefs rare,

" I ceafed at length to be the *public care.* (*g*)

" Yet being refolved thro' all mankind to rove,

" I, when neglected, proffered love for love ; (*h*)

" And tho' an Earl's Coronet I ftill poffeft,

" *Corona Veneris* (*i*) was my favourite Creft."

She paufed ; when SATAN, with decifion

    nice,

Deemed thefe but petty-larcenies in vice ;

She pilfered from herfelf, fhe injured none,

And therefore was unfit to grace his throne.

                    " Thy

(*g*) *Publica cura*—an expreffion made ufe of by Horace, for a Courtefan, L. II. Od. 8.

(*b*) This was apparently the cafe at a late Mafque-rade.

(*i*) This is not the Myrtle Wreath with which the *Venus Amica* crowns her Votaries, but a certain *Frontlet*, with which her Baftard Sifter, the *Venus Meretrix*, is ufed to ftigmatize her Devotees.

" Thy deeds have been fo very mean, he cried,

" They but prefer you to be * * 's bride : (k)

" Befides, to credit your firft Shame we're loath,

" As being acquitted on a *Bible-Oath*." (l)

The next that rofe was wanton * * *,

With front affured, and dreffed *en Cavalier :*

A * * * (m) led her forth, *Jack H* * * * (n)
    followed,

While Grooms and Jockeys in full chorus hal-
   looed.

The tale fhe told 'twere needlefs to repeat,

'Twas Meffalina's hiftory compleat ;

         She

(k) See The Diaboliad, page 31, 2d paragraph.

(l) The Story is upon record, and therefore requires no note.

(m) A foreign Count with whom fhe had her firft *fublic* amour.

(n) A poftilion with whom fhe had her fecond.

She loved to ride, and to be ridden too,
And came prepared to *give the Devil his due.*

Old * * (*o*) trembled at such vigorous boast,
And quick dismissed her from the Stygian
    coast.
To * *'s Case in point, (*p*) he thus alludes,
" *Rough Riders*, male or female, HELL ex-
" cludes."

Then with a high and all-commanding air,
Slowly advancing, * * *, once fair,
Appeared in distant view. The Cyprian Dame,
Escorted by her MARS, (*q*) aspired to claim

                  The

(*o*) See the Diaboliad, last page, and last line.

(*p*) See the Diaboliad, p. 31, first paragraph.

(*q*) We confess ourselves to be in doubt whether
the Poet alludes to general C*, or to the Secretary at
War, in this passage.

The vacant Crown; but haply on her way,
Perceiving in a nook some Imps at play,
She turned aside, to learn some sleight of hand,
To cut, or shuffle, and the game command;
Some new device, some yet-unpractised cheat,
To cozen, pilfer, and the Rook compleat.

* * * * * * * * * * *

* * * * * * * * * *

This gave advantage to a rival Quean
To take her place, and prior audience gain.

* * now pressed before, and claimed desert,
For having broke a too fond husband's heart;
Yet to the joys of marriage-rites still true,
Ere one was dead, she had engaged with
      two:
The first she jilted, being thought too tame,
Preferred the Bully of her ticklish fame,

                And

And like *Quiteria* in *Cervantes'* Tale,

The bleeding *Bafil* wed, *Camacho* (r) left to

    rail:

✻ ✻ ✻ ✻ ✻ ✻ ✻ ✻ ✻ ✻

✻ ✻ ✻ ✻ ✻ ✻ ✻ ✻ ✻ ✻ ✻

But timorous * *, in a fore affright,

Hearing the defperate prowefs of her Knight,

Replied, " I dare not to this match agree,

" Who fights my Priefts, (s) would *play the*

    " *Devil* with me."

                        Then

(r) And his railing has had good effect, we hear, as the Don has got ten thoufand pieces, and a good riddance into the bargain, for a releafe of contract. This is the fecond Suitor this Heroine bought off. The firft was one to whom fhe had been affianced by her father's will, and who pioufly attending to the advice of Solomon, *Leave off Contention before it be meddled with,* remitted his claim upon that Condition.

(s) This alludes to a late extraordinary Duel; but

Then next moved forward, waddling on her
    ftumps,

A weight to put poor Atlas to his trumps ;

A Dame that late had puzzled heraldry

To fay what *Alias* it fhould ftile her by ;

Who, had fhe been but born in days of
    yore,

Would have given Hercules one labour more;

For fure no mortal Might for her was able,

But his who cleanfed the foul Augean Stable.

                              By

we cannot fee why the Poet has taken the liberty of
putting the Noun into the Plural Number here; for
the Member of the Church Militant in that martial
ftrife, is but one; and we cannot fuppofe our Author
meant to compliment him with the name of *Legion*—
Nor is that Reverend Perfon yet in poffeffion of *Plu-
ralities*, either. In our Second Edition perhaps we
may be able to explain this matter further.

By Nature wanton, falfe, and prone to ill,

Beauty fhe had, and wicked wit at will;

Confiftent ftill in Vice, from firft to laft,

Thro fcenes of *many-coloured* (*t*) life fhe paft.

Not brooking long in amorous flames to
       burn,

She whored or wedded, as it ferved her
       turn;

She married and unmarried as fhe pleafed,

While Lords (*u*) and Doctors Commons ftood
       amaz'd!

But now grown wifer, fhe refolv'd to fix

Her feat of empire on the banks of Styx;

              F   But

(*t*) An Epithet of Doctor Johnfon's, in his Prologue to the opening of Drury-Lane Theatre.

(*u*) The Houfe of Lords.

But firſt enquired, " Are any here who knew

" A Devil on Earth, whom Men call *Le*

    Boiteux ? (*x*)

" For vengeance on him, *even to Hell's-*

    " *gates* (*y*) I come ;

" And know, my Liege, I'm juſt arrived

    " from Rome : (*z*)

                       " On

(*x*) Our Ariſtophanes, or *Devil upon Two Sticks*, with whom this Lady held a ſort of Mountebank Cor-reſpondence, upon the occaſion of a Piece of his then coming out, in which ſome part of her *private* hiſtory of *public* notoriety, was to be exhibited on the ſtage.

(*y*) The Author, we ſuppoſe, meant here to allude to one of her Letters upon the above occaſion ; but he is miſtaken in the paſſage ; the Lady did not promiſe to carry her complaiſance ſo far. As well as we can recollect, ſhe only mentioned that ſhe would attend him *to Tyburn*, and then leave him to ſhift for himſelf, and *go to the Devil his own way.*

(*z*) She had lately a villa near that City, and lived in great intimacy with the Pope.

" On earth he made my Hell; and have
　　　" not I,

" As Satan's Queen, (*a*) a right to make
　　　" him fry ?

" What mufic to my ears, to hear him
　　　" yell,

" And make his *Trip to Calais*, (*b*) one to
　　　" Hell !

" Above he 'fcaped my utmoft fpite and
　　　" power,

" Grant me revenge, I afk no other Dower !

　　　　　　F 2　　　　　　" And

(*a*) This expreffion was rather premature—She
was but prefumptive Confort. But, perhaps, fhe
thought fhe might do in Hell as fhe had done on
Earth, and marry whom fhe pleafed, right or wrong.

(*b*) This Piece was afterwards reprefented; but
whether through fear, favour, or fee, was fo garbled,
as foon to fink into oblivion.

" And reft my Suit for juftice, on this
　　" hope,

" That I am recommended by the Pope." (*c*)

Who faw and heard her pleading, muft con-
　　fefs,

Sh' had *Falftaff's* flefh, and wit, and wicked-
　　nefs ;

Tho' fome there were who thought her wanton
　　plight

Refembled more *Doll Tear - Sheet,* than the
　　Knight.

　　　　　　　　　　　　　　　　Yet

(*c*) Thefe two Potentates have ever been in ftrict
confederacy together; and his infallible Holinefs has
fent more fouls to SATAN's empire, by his *pardons,*
abfolutions and indulgences, than ever were difpatched
thither from the *Scaffold or the Gallows.*

Yet SATAN cried, " Thy claim I muſt
    deny,

" For want of one Vice more, Hypocri-
    " ſy ; *(d)*

" Your barefaced Sinners are not worth my
    " notice,

" Demure pretending Saints, *hoc eſt in vo-*
    " *tis. (e)*

                      " Then

(*d*) This was the anſwer of the late Lord Cheſter-
field, to a profligate Parſon who was recommended
to him as a Chaplain, once, when he was going
Ambaſſador to *The States.* There were ſcandalous
perſons in thoſe times, it ſeems, as well as in the preſent ones.

(*e*) This is a Sentence from Horace, but falſely
quoted.—The Verb Subſtantive *Sum* is in the preter-
imperfect tenſe there, but turned into the preſent time
here. This is one of the vices of verſe, which, like the
tyranny of Procruſtes, lengthens or ſhortens the mem-
                           bers,

" Then back return, re - wed your former
    " Peer,

" And tafte an Hell on earth, ere you come
    " here."

    The Court was now difturbed.   A jovial
    troop

Of female libertines appeared *en groupe* ;

O——, B————, E——, B————,

H————, T————, and a Hundred more ;

Which noify Amazons made fuch a riot,

That SATAN thought 't had been a Polifh
    Diet.

                        " Zounds !"

bers, according as they fuit its own meafure.   But
poffibly our Author, who is an adept in metaphyfics,
may reply, that there is no diftinction of times or
tenfes, in the Region of Spirits—the paft, the prefent,
and the future being all the inftant *now*, among immor-
tal beings.

" Zounds !" quoth he, in a rage, " whence

    " this abuse ?

" Call up my guards—What ! is all Hell broke

    " loose ?"

The deafened Cryer thrice proclaimed, *O Yes !*

And Imps and Implings (*f*) gave a general

    hiss.

Silence at last obtained, each strove to

    shew

Her several right *to rule the roast below* ;

              'Till

(*f*) We have looked for this diminutive of a diminutive, in Johnson's Dictionary, in vain.—We are,
therefore, at a loss for sufficient authority to support the
word, except we may suppose it an allusion to the
vulgar expression, which is sometimes applied to a
demure Sinner, *that be is as innocent as a Devil of
Two Years old.*

'Till SATAN tired with prate, thus made
  reply ;
" Your claims fo like, and equal are, that I
" Can fee no choice, except Polygamy :
" But when my future Queen takes ftate upon
  " her,
" Ye fhall be all preferred to—*Maids of Ho-*
  " *nour.*" (g)

  The fcene now fhifted, on the ftage ap-
    pears
The Sock and Bufkin Heroines, linked in
    pairs;

            B——

(*g*) Here the Devil feems to have been a little out,
in the point of Etiquette; for as this illuftrious groupe
are all Matrons, he could only appoint them as *Ladies
of the Bed Chamber.*

B—— and Y—— firſt trail the purple train;

Next A—— and B—— intervene,

'Twixt Y—— and B———, who cloſe the

Scene.

Their Plea was modeſt, which is ſomething

rare,

In any Modern male or female Player; *(h)*

For, not preſuming on their own demerits,

Their puny Vices, in this land of *ſpi-*

rits,

They only claim'd, that having acted Queens

On COVENT GARDEN and old DRURY's

ſcenes,

      And

(*h*) Our Author's Sarcaſm here is, in general, too
true; for we know but few exceptions to the re-
mark.

And being *Shadows*, in the mimic ſhow,

Their rank they challenged in the *Shades* be-

    below;

And thought themſelves intitled to obtain

An equal dignity in PLUTO's reign. (*i*)

SATAN, who has wit and humour, if he'd

    ſhew it,

(For who but him made ROCHESTER a

    Poet ?

                                Or

(*i*) A poetical licence again! See our former Note,
upon a ſimilar paſſage, in p. 2. But probably the Author meant to be critical, in this place, by making a
diſtinction here between the imaginary Tartarus of the
Pagan Creed, and the real Hell of the Chriſtian Be-
lief. In the firſt, Souls were but *Shadows*, which was
too metaphyſical a notion to ſway the multitude. But
the latter doctrine tells us, that we ſhall *pick up our
Crumbs* again at the day of judgment, in order to receive *corporal puniſhment*. This is ſenſible, ſubſtantial,
and edifying.

Or who the Author of the *Henriade* (k)

Infpired to write the filthy *Pucellade ?* (*l*)

Or inftigated the *Diabolade)?* (*m*)

Thus, with a fly, Sardonic fmile, replied:

" Your claim, fair Puppets, muft be here de-

" nied;

" For

(*k*) M. Voltaire.

(*l*) *La Pucelle d' Orleans*, or, the Maid of Orleans.

(*m*) *The Diabolade*, for The *Diabolia?*. The firft fhould have been the Title, by all rules of Derivation. 'Tis a Subftantive, and the latter is an Adjective. Diabolia*dus, da, dum*. Befides the juftnefs of the alteration in the Word, our Author might have had a further intereft in it, alfo, as his own Title of *Diabo-Lady* derives more fairly from one word than the other.

" For hear a truth, a truth for once I'll tell :

" Whate'er your ftate, while yet on earth ye

"   " dwell,

" Your Green-room Dolls are *Kitchen Maids*

"   " in Hell." (*n*)

At length with dimpling cheek, and leering

    eye,

Long noted in the rolls of Infamy,

* * ftept forth and claim'd the vacant crown,

For every crime that bears in Hell renown.

                                    Her

(*n*) This is meant in Oppofition to *Maids of Honour*,
above-mentioned; as he did not think their ftation or
character in life, entitled them to any higher office
in the Houfehold of the *Pandemonium*.

Her argument she thus maintained with force,

Recounting deeds of ' blame from bad to
    worse :

" Tho' blest with beauty, rank, and powers to
    engage,

" To charm in Youth, and win *Time-honour'd* (o)
    age ;

" Yet still ambitious of a nobler aim,

" I squandered beauty, dignity, and fame,

" To earn thy notice, thy loved Empire own,

" And, *jure infernali*, share thy throne—

" False to my husband's bed, I scorned to
    rove

" Thro' common guilt, but chose incestuous
    " love ;

                                    " I drove

(o) An Epithet borrowed from Shakespeare, in Rich-
ard II.

" I drove him to diftraction and defpair,

" And then *removed* a Sifter and her heir;

" To make Succeffion fure, and feal the deed,

" Which helped my fpurious iffue to fuc-

  " ceed (*p*)

* * * * * * * * * * * *

* * * * * * * * * * *

" Of favours profligate and nothing nice,

" In many another mean ignoble vice;

      " I gamboled,

(*p*) This is an old Story; and we confefs that we agree in the fame Charity with the good old Woman, who, hearing of *the Paffion*, one Sunday at Church, faid, that, *as it was fo long ago, fhe hoped in the Lord that it was not true.*

" I gamboled, and I gambled deep at play,

" And raised finances in less legal way ;

" I *sweated gold*, (*q*) and practised every
   " cheat,

" Which, known to thee, I need not here
    " repeat.

" My deeds with thine compared, in every
    " art,

" Prove me in all—thy worthy counterpart :

" In fine, to crown my merits, you shall find

" I'm the reverse of her you left behind :

" Nay more, to shew me fit to share thy
    " sway,

" Behold, my Liege, my locks, like thine, are
   " grey. (*r*)

         " Father

(*q*) Another obsolete Story.

(*r*) See the Diaboliad, page 47.

" Father of Lies! accept my proffered hand,

" What richer portion canſt thou now de-
" mand;

" For e'en to all the Ruſſias ſhou'dſt thou·
" rove,

" I equal CATHERINE, both in hate and
" love;

" And werc SEMIRAMIS herſelf alive,

" With her in deeds of darkneſs I dare ſtrive."

The liſtening Imps with wonder ſtood
amazed,

And at each period ſubtler ſulphur blazed;

While at a diſtance, on the Elyſian Plains,

Where even the Bleſt re-act their former
ſcenes

Of mortal life, was ſeen in geſture wild,

A mournful Mother weeping o'er her child. (s)

.   The

(s) See page 77, Line 10.

'The aſtoniſh'd Court ſat ſilent all the while,

SATAN *grinned horrible a ghaſtly ſmile* ; (*t*)

Then cried, "Reſolved — I ſwear by Sacred

"Styx,

" On thy alliance my firm choice I fix."

'The nuptial torches yield a brimſtone flame,

And Heralds are commanded to proclaim,

With Ætna's thunders, and infernal Yell,

⸺⸺⸺ is crowned unrivalled Queen of Hell!"

(*t*) *Grinned horribly,* &c.   MILTON.

F   I   N   I   S.